one Hungry Dragon

by Julie Wenzlick

Illustrated by Mary Beningo

ISBN-13: 978-09978925-6-7
Published by Wordmeister Press

For Annabelle and Maisie

May you always be as brave and clever as you already are.
Love, Grammie

For Lauren and Joey

I hope you always stay kids at heart.
Love, Mommy

There once lived a dragon whose lair was a cave
And no one nearby liked the way he behaved.

At six every day when the clock struck the hour
He called for a maiden that he could devour!

When townsfolk refused and instead brought him meat.
He whined and complained and breathed flames at their feet.

It wasn't that maidens were what he preferred
He knew he should want one...or so he had heard

(But deep down the dragon just wanted good food.
A maiden—for dinner—would simply be rude!)

He had folks believing he would eat a maiden
So everyone looked for new ways to dissuade him.

The cooks of the kingdom tried hard to appease him,
Preparing fine foods they felt certain would please him.

Like pasta and pancakes and raspberry pie
Zucchini, linguini, pastrami on rye.

He tasted each item with dragon-like care
But each morsel burned when he merely breathed air.

The one dragon trait he had struggled to learn
Was how to eat food without having it burn.

He longed for his youth—
back before he breathed fire
When flavorful foods
filled his every desire.

He sighed and he paced
   and he opened his mouth
And burned down the trees
   from the north to the south.

The villagers knew
   they could not ask a maiden
To offer herself
   to this ravenous dragon!

Yet night after night
   he did not eat his dinner.
The dragon, still hungry,
   grew thinner and thinner.

The princess, meanwhile, observed from afar
And noticed his food always ended up charred.

This poor hungry dragon was skinny and boney.
She sensed that his threats to eat maidens were phony

She spotted his tears
    and could feel his frustration
She thought of a plan—
    it was sheer inspiration!

She traded her princess's gown for a sack.
She dirtied her face and put on a boy's cap.

She stopped off in town
    for a large ice cream cone.
Proceeding due north,
    she then ventured alone.

The dragon lay sleeping. Slight flames there arose.
She watched as the fire shot out of his nose.
"Hey Dragon," she whispered, "I've brought you a treat.
It's not a fair maiden, but something else sweet.
"Just try it, you'll like it—it cannot be burned.
It's cold and it's creamy—it's ice that's been churned!"

The maiden seemed thoughtful and ever so sweet.
In one giant gulp he then swallowed her treat.
A cool feeling rushed from his head to his toes.
His once-constant flames did not shoot from his nose.

"It's ice cream!" she shouted.
"Your fire's gone out!
You cannot burn ice cream!
It's frozen throughout!"

The flames were not coming,
    not even a speck.
The now happy dragon
    stretched out his long neck.

"Whoopee!" cried the dragon.
"Now food will taste great!
I'll savor each flavor.
  My gosh, I can't wait!"

The princess—so joyful—
  ripped off her disguise.
She hugged her new friend,
  who had tears in his eyes.

The dragon, ashamed
  that she ever had feared him,
Respected her courage
  to even come near him.

He gobbled up ice cream and snow cones all day
While firemen smiled and cried out, "Hurray!"

The kingdom was safe now,
for maidens and trees
A dragon—not hungry—
is easy to please!

At festival time though, he relights his flames
To grill tasty burgers amidst picnic games.
Of all of the foods that he now finds so yummy
Ice cream's still his favorite----just look at his tummy!

About the Author

Julie Wenzlick, a retired English teacher, conceived the idea for *One Hungry Dragon* in fourth grade, when she wrote the original version for her elementary school newspaper. Over 50 years later, she revived the idea and paired with illustrator Mary Beningo, one of her former high school students, to at long last publish this tale. Julie's other books include: *Santa's Dilemma: To Eat or Not to Eat*; *The Day Annabelle was Bitten by a Doodlebug*; and *The Day Maisie Picked a Daisy*. She has created songs to go with each story, and is now enjoying her visits to local classrooms where she shares the stories and songs with students. She hopes to inspire many young people to write stories of their own. Find her books on www.juliewenzlick.com

About the Illustrator

Mary Beningo is an artist, art teacher, wife and mommy of two little kidlets. Teaching youngsters to be creative is one of her favorite things to do, aside from spending time with her family. She enjoys drawing and painting all kinds of artwork for children. Mary earned a bachelor's degree from Central Michigan University and a master's degree in Visual Art Education from Western Michigan University. This is her first time illustrating a children's book and she hopes to illustrate more books in the future. Mary lives in Michigan with her funny husband Andy and her imaginative children, Lauren and Joey.

Made in the USA
Lexington, KY
15 September 2017